Mini Rabbit

NOT
LOST

FOR
EVIE
&
OTTO
x

First published in hardback by HarperCollins *Children's Books* in 2018
First published in paperback in 2019

3 5 7 9 10 8 6 4 2

ISBN: 978–0–00–826484–0

HarperCollins *Children's Books* is a division of HarperCollins*Publishers* Ltd.

Text and illustrations copyright © John Bond 2018
Cover illustration copyright © John Bond 2019

Visit our website at: www.harpercollins.co.uk

Printed and bound in Italy by Rotolito S.p.A.

Mini Rabbit

NOT
LOST

JOHN BOND

HarperCollins *Children's Books*

Mini Rabbit and Mother Rabbit
are making a cake.

Mini Rabbit likes cake.

Caaaaake!

Oh dear, it looks like they've run out of berries.

Hang on,
Mini Rabbit!
There are some
under the . . .

Too late.
Mini Rabbit is off.

Must have cake.

Cake   Cake

Cake!

I can find berries.

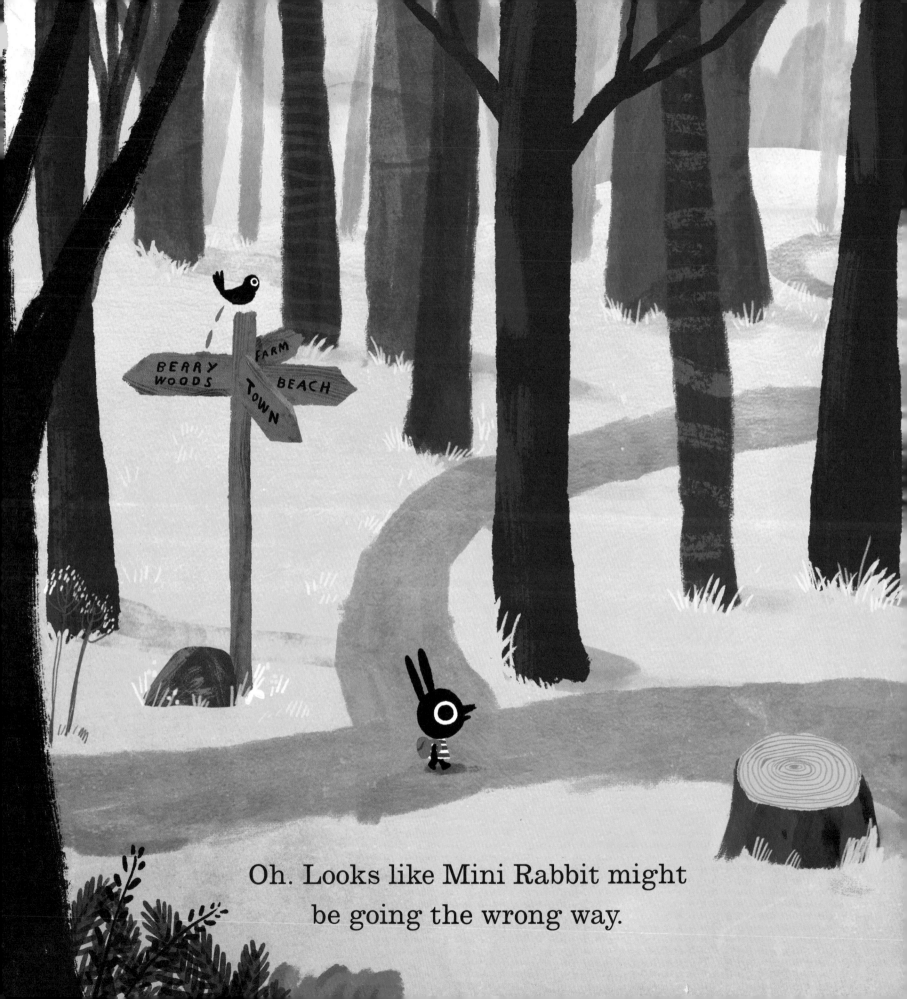

Oh. Looks like Mini Rabbit might
be going the wrong way.

Hello, Mini Rabbit.
Where are you going?
Do you need any help?

No, thank you.
Don't need help.
Looking for berries.
Making a cake.

Cake

Cake

Cake!

260-6

Where could Mini Rabbit be going now?

I
can
find
berries.

Maybe this chap can help
Mini Rabbit find berries?

Hello, Mini Rabbit.
It's pretty cold out here.
Don't you need
your coat?

No, no.
Not cold.
Looking for berries.
Making a cake.

Mini Rabbit has definitely gone the wrong way now ...

And it looks very dangerous up here!

Mini Rabbit, STOP!
You're far too small
to go down there,
aren't you?

No, no.
Not too small.
Looking for berries.
Making a ...

Cake.

Cake...

Cake...

"

Not sure this is a good place for Mini Rabbit to find berries.

Poor Mini Rabbit.

SNIFF
SNIFF

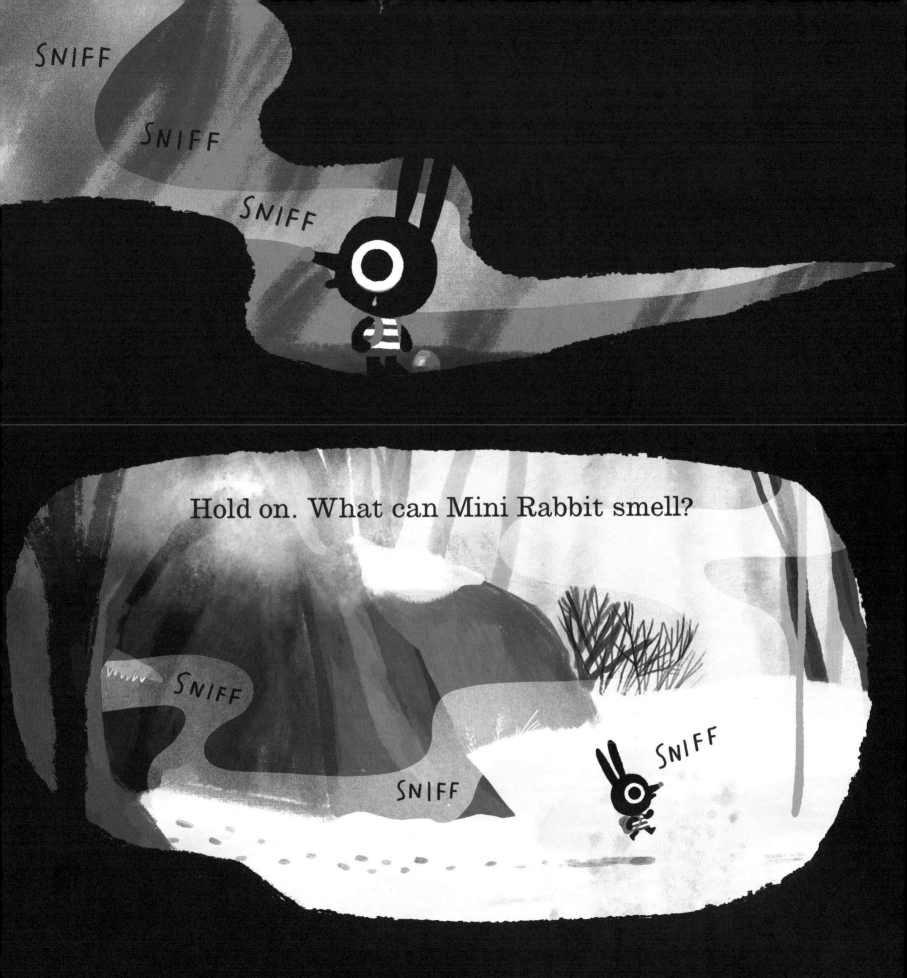

Hold on. What can Mini Rabbit smell?

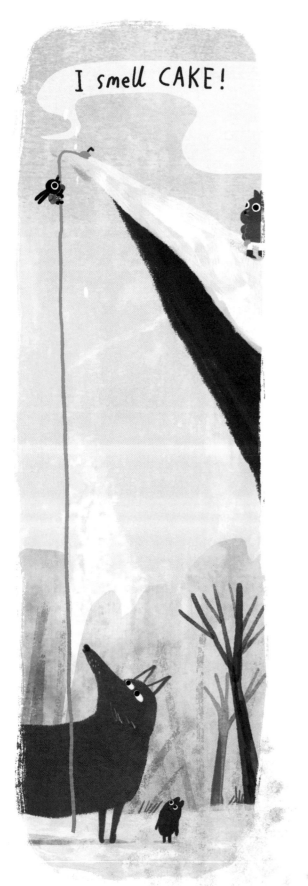

Berry cake berry cake berry cake...

I found a berry!

And I'm going...

Mother Rabbit looks very pleased to see Mini Rabbit.

There you are!

I found a berry.

Well done,
Mini Rabbit.

Now, would you like
some cake?